MW00768429

I'm Just the Right Size
ISBN 1-59185-461-X

Requests for information may be addressed to:

The children's book imprint of Strang Communications Company
600 Rinehart Rd., Lake Mary, FL 32746
www.charismakids.com

Children's Editor: Pat Matuszak
Designed by Granite Design

Printed in China
04 05 06 07 — 5 4 3 2 1

I'm Just the Right Size

A CharismaLife Story

Illustrated by
Dan Foote

Craig the Crab lived in a kingdom of sea creatures in a beautiful land under the water called Discovery Cove. He was smaller—a lot smaller; he thought—than most of the crabs his age.

Rocky was Craig's best friend. They had lots of other friends who lived in the cove—seahorses, rays, sharks and fish of all kinds.

King Crab was the king of Discovery Cove. He thought all the creatures that lived there together were special. He helped them use their talents to help make it the best place to live.

One day, Craig and Rocky headed for the park. They wanted to go to the big Seaweed Festival where all their friends would be playing games. As soon as they got there, Rocky and Craig jumped in line. They wanted to get picked for the best team in clamball.

One by one, the players were chosen by the captains. Only three creatures were left in the line—Craig, a slow sea turtle, and a small girl cowfish.

"But we only need one more player," called Sheldon Starfish. "I pick you, Wendy Cowfish. Get in line with my team."

"Aw, I didn't want to play anyway..." Craig said. But he looked sad even though he tried to act like it didn't matter.

Inside, he felt a little lump of hurt drop to the bottom of his heart.

Shelly was the slow turtle who wasn't chosen for a team. She looked at Craig's sad face. She felt worse for him than for herself:

"Hey, Craig, maybe we're not the biggest or the best athletes. But that doesn't mean we aren't special or important.

King Crab told me that God made us all special. He said we all have a purpose—something we are created to do.

He said not to worry about all the things I can't do.

He said I should look around and find things I can do to help others."

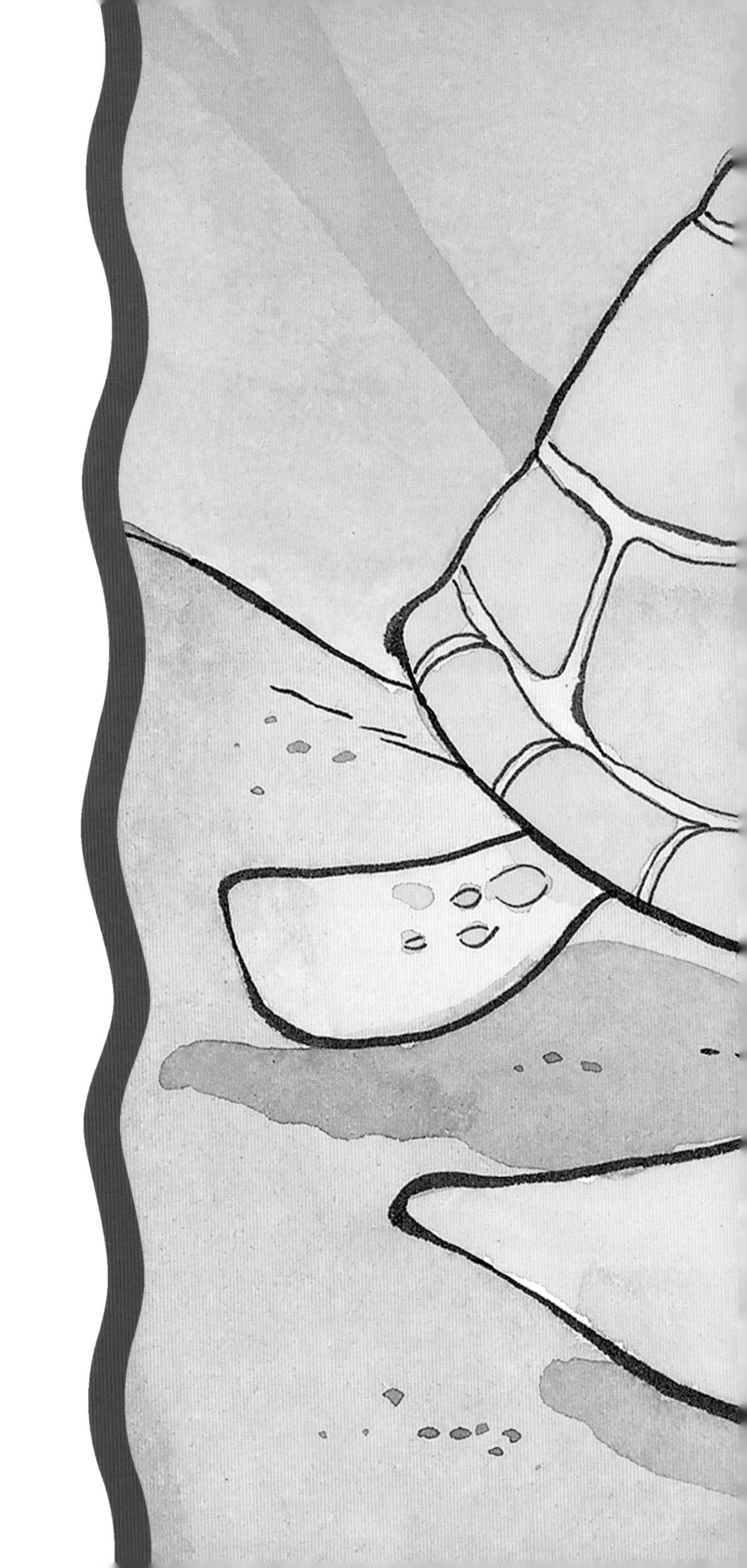

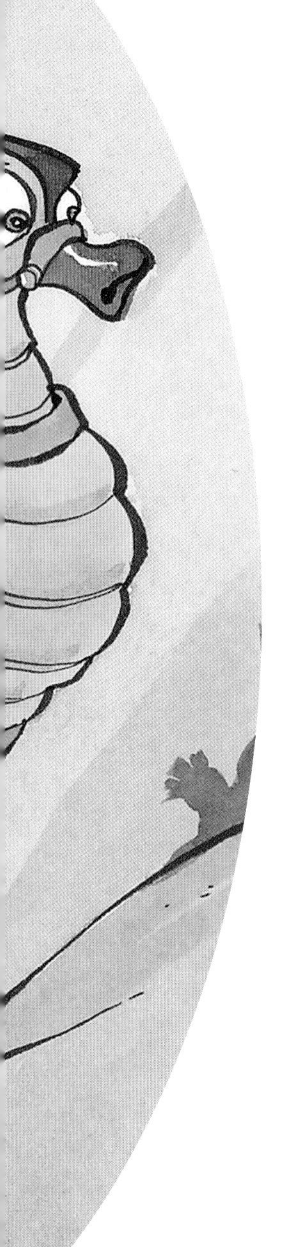

Just then they heard the neighing of seahorses!

King Crab drove up in his clamshell chariot and called out:

"Come here, everyone! I have an important announcement.

Our kingdom is under attack by a giant octopus!

I have come up with a plan to trap him. I need a brave helper to go with me."

All the creatures rushed up to the front of the crowd to be chosen to be his helper. They would do anything for the king and their families in the Cove. And they all wanted to be in on an exciting adventure.

Craig wanted to be chosen, but he put his head down and sidestepped away. “I’m not the tallest, smartest, or anything special...” Poor Craig felt like digging a hole and hiding in it.

King Crab looked around the crowd carefully, “I need someone who is a very special size...”

All the sea creatures stood as tall as they could.

Craig put his chin on his claws. “Well, that leaves me out. I’ll never be the one to be picked if size is important.”

Just then King Crab pointed right at Craig and shouted:

“I want YOU to help me, Craig Crab! You are just the right size!”

“ME?” squeaked Craig.

“Him?” laughed Big Bubba Blowfish. “He’s way too little to fight a giant octopus.”

“Not true,” smiled King Crab. “Craig is the perfect size to help me carry out my plan.”

Craig was so excited to be chosen. "I'll be happy to help!" he said.

The king showed Craig a trap he had made using an old bottle and a large fishing net. "Here's the plan, my brave friend," King Crab explained, "You don't have to fight the octopus yourself. You just hide in the bottle. When he tries to pull you out, we will drop the net on him. Once he is trapped inside it, our kingdom will be safe!"

"So, I'm just the bait!" cried Craig.

"Don't worry," the king assured him. "You'll be safe if you just follow my directions: Stay deep inside the bottle. Old octopus won't be able to reach you.

"All the other crabs are too big to fit inside the bottle. This special job is the perfect one for you."

Craig started pacing outside the bottle, waiting for the octopus to swim by. For the first time in his life, he was happy to be small!

And he understood that God had other things planned for him besides playing clamball. He felt proud to serve the king and protect his friends.

Suddenly, a shadow passed over him. The silent octopus was sneaking up on him. He scurried away toward the bottle. His little feet tried as hard as they could to run into the opening. But it felt like he was going in slow motion.

The octopus was closing in on him. He felt one of its tentacles swirl out into the water.

He popped into the bottle just in time. Then, Craig did as the king had told him. He ran all the way to the back of the bottle, so the octopus couldn't reach him.

As the enemy tried to reach into Craig's hiding place, the king and his army dropped the net over him.

Old octopus was trapped by the strong net and there was nothing he could do to free himself.

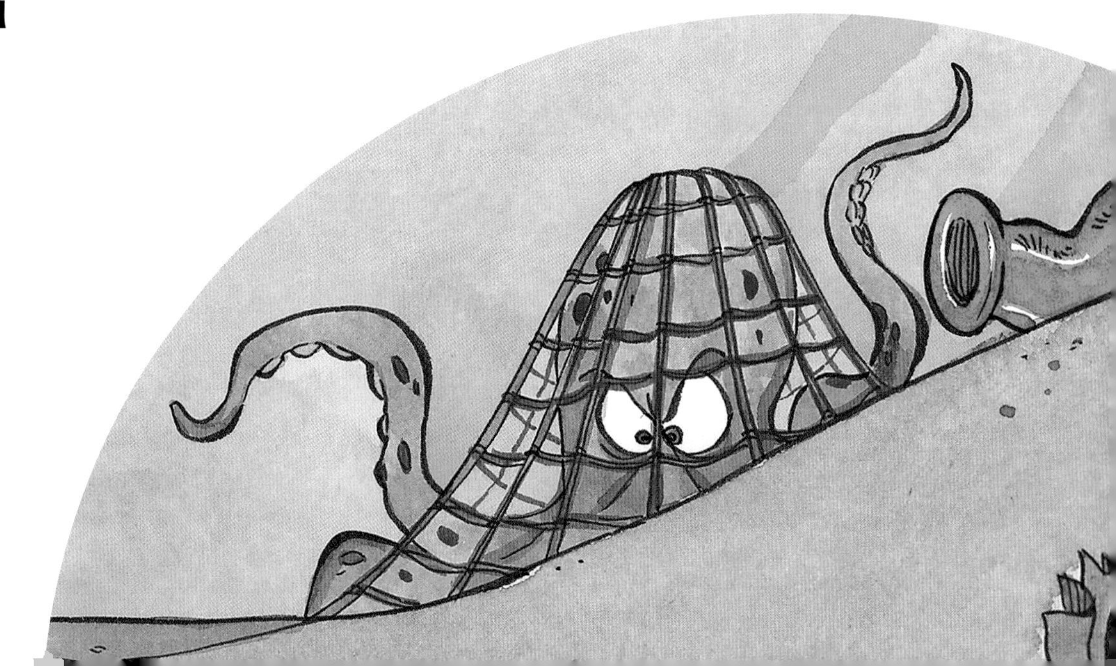

Craig crawled out of the bottle and the king rushed over and thanked him: "Job well done, son! You did everything just the way you were created by God to do it. Don't ever let anyone tell you that you are too small. In this kingdom, everyone is special.

"And everyone is just the right size."

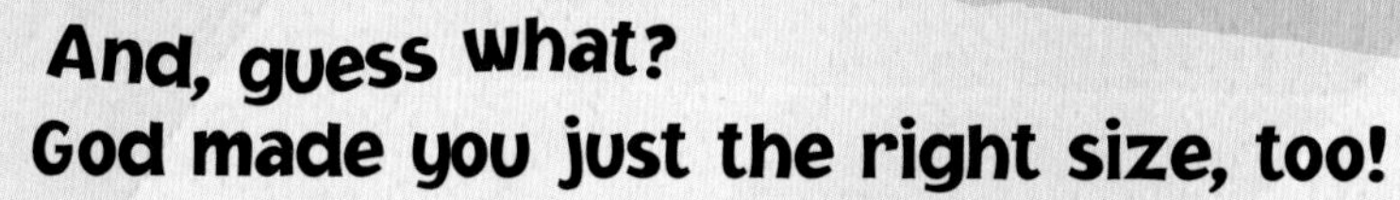

And, guess what?
God made you just the right size, too!

He has a special plan for your life, just like the king had a special plan for Craig.

He gave you talents so you can help others, too.

Do you want to be God's helper? Just talk to him in prayer and tell him. Then look around and see what you can do, like Shelly the Seaturtle told Craig to do. Your family and friends will be blessed when you are willing to be a blessing.

And you will find a job that is just the right size for you!